T0198808

The Punishment

Andre Jamiro Lee Sr.

Illustrations by Kenn Yapsangco

To order additional copies of this book, contact:
Xlibris
844-714-8691
www.Xlibris.com
Orders@Xlibris.com

ISBN: Softcover 978-1-4797-5856-2

Library of Congress Control Number: 2012922634

Print information available on the last page.

I would like to dedicate this book to my mom and dad, to my teachers, coaches and the United States Military for teaching me the discipline that I needed to live my life and raise three great kids with my wife Mary.

In the game of poker each player is dealt a set of cards, and by the set of cards that are dealt and the way they are played determines the outcome of the game. In life we all have choices to make. The choices we make determine how we live our lives. The choices we make have consequences, some good and some bad. For instance, there was this young couple who lived in a small town called Maple Hill, North Carolina. They wanted to start a new family, but before they did they promised each other to spare the rod when it came time to punish their child. A few months later the young man and his young wife had a healthy baby boy.

As time went by, their child got older, smarter, and started to misbehave. He learned just what he could and could not get away with. The young boy started to steal from his mom and dad, but the young couple would only just tell the young boy not to do it anymore. The young boy started school and it wasn't long before he started to misbehave.

He started to steal from the other children. The principal would ask the young boy if he stole anything knowing that the young boy did, but the young boy would just lie and say no. When the principal called the young couple and told them their son was seen stealing at school the young couple was in disbelief and would take the side of their son.

As the years went by the young couple and the young boy got older. The young boy is now a teenager and full of spunk! A while later the young boy started hanging with a street gang (just a bunch of young punks). One day the young teenager and the street gang went to the corner store on the other side of town to shop lift. The store owner was not new to these children. They always came around to start trouble and steal candy, chips and soda pop.

Most of the time the shop owner would just run them off with a stick, but this time as the shop owner chased the bad teens off one of them had tripped and hurt his leg. The shop owner ran over to help the young teen and just then he recognized the young teen. It was the kid from just up the street from where he lived. The shop owner said, "Hey I know you." The first thing the teen said was that he was not trying to steal anything and that he was not with the group of teens.

The shop owner did not believe the teen and took him home to his mom and dad. When the shop owner told the young boy's mom and dad what the young teen had done, the young teen just denied everything. The shop keeper said to the young teen, "Tell the truth boy. The truth will set you free!" But the teen just stuck to his lies, and the shop owner in discuss left the boy with his mom and dad and went home.

Years went by. Summer turned to fall, fall to winter, and winter to spring. The boy grew and so did his appetite for stealing. One day the young man and some of his friends tried to rob the corner store. The young men thought it would be an easy steal, but they did not know that the store owner had started keeping a shot gun behind his counter. The young men ran in the store with a gun, and yelled at the shop owner, "Give me all your money or else." The shop owner was so afraid he gave them all the money he had. As the young men started to run out the door,

the shop owner grabbed his shot gun, and fired a single shot. One of the young men went down bleeding profusely from the neck and leg. The shot had hit the main artery in the young man's leg. The store owner ran over to help the young man and just then a feeling of déjà vu came over the store owner. He grabbed the young man. The young man tried to say something but no words could come out. The old store owner held the young man like a new born baby and looked at him. He recognized the young man as the boy he caught stealing as a kid. The old store owner started crying saying "why, why, why." The young man died in his arms.

Later that evening, police went to the address of the young man to inform his mother and father of the death of their son. The officer knocked on the hard wood doors and the old lady came to the door and said, "Yes can I help you officer?" The officer said, "We hate to inform you that your son has been shoot and killed earlier in an attempted robbery. We offer our condolences." The old lady loudly cried out for God and dropped to her knees. The officers held the old lady as her husband came to comfort her. The officers explained everything to the old man and left the home.

Later that Sunday evening after the funeral, the parents were at home eating there Sunday dinner. There was a knock on the door. The old man got up to answer the door. As he opened the large hard wood doors a strong cold wind blew into the house. Just then along flew a huge black bird into the house. It frightened the old man and lady, but soon the large black bird flew out the house. They finished their meal and got ready for bed.

Later that night as the old man and his wife slept, the old lady felt someone tugging at her foot. She sat up in the bed and saw a silhouette of a young man. The old lady reached over and tapped the old man on the leg. The old man set up and asked his wife, "What is going on?" The old lady said, "look," and pointed at the silhouette of a young man. Just then a familiar voice came from the silhouette. It was the voice of their son. The old lady said, "It is our son. He is not dead!" The voice replied, "Mom and Dad this is the spirit of your son and my body is dead."

I have come to show you something so you can share with others. The spirit said, "Mom and Dad please follow me." The spirit of the young man lead the old man and his wife to a round clearing in the forest where there were two trees. One large tree and one small tree in the center of the round clearing in the forest. "See Mom and Dad," the spirit said. "Do you see these two trees one small and the other large? These trees are me at different parts of my life when I was growing up. See this big tree is all ready grown and I can't bend it or make it grow either way. It has already grown into it's own way. This is me when I was grown and corrupt. You see this little tree you can bend it that way and it will grow that way or you can bend it this way and it will grow this way. See Mom and Dad when I was younger you chose to spare the rod and doing so spoiled the child. I had no discipline and no respect for others or their property." The spirit pulled the little tree out of the ground and striped all the branches off it and turned to his Mom and Dad and said, "This is what you should have done to me when I was younger."

Printed in the United States
by Baker & Taylor Publisher Services